# The Jungle Book

# The Jungle Book

by Rudyard Kipling
adapted by Diane Wright Landolf
illustrated by John Rowe

## A STEPPING STONE BOOK™

Random House 🏠 New York

Text copyright © 2008 by Diane Wright Landolf.
Illustrations copyright © 2008 by John Rowe.

Visit us on the Web!
www.steppingstonesbooks.com
www.randomhouse.com/kids

Educators and librarians, for a variety of teaching tools, visit us at
www.randomhouse.com/teachers

*Library of Congress Cataloging-in-Publication Data*
Landolf, Diane Wright.
The jungle book / by Rudyard Kipling ; adapted by Diane Wright Landolf ; illustrated by John Rowe. — 1st ed.
    p.    cm.
"A Stepping Stone Book."
Summary: Adaptation of Rudyard Kipling's "The Jungle Book," focusing on stories that feature Mowgli, Baloo the bear, and Bagheera the panther.
ISBN 978-0-375-84276-4 (pbk.) — ISBN 978-0-375-94062-0 (lib. bdg.)
[1. Jungles—Fiction. 2. Animals—Fiction. 3. India—Fiction.] I. Kipling, Rudyard, 1865–1936. Jungle book. II. Rowe, John, ill. III. Title.
PZ7.L2317345Ju 2008    [Fic]—dc22    2007021738

Printed in the United States of America    10 9 8 7 6 5 4
First Edition

*For Mom, Marcia, and Kristin*
*—D.W.L.*

*For Monica, Julia, and Johnny—wife, daughter, and son*
*—J.R.*

# Chapter 1

Far away in India was a cave in the hills where a wolf family lived. Just before the sun set, Father Wolf woke up to hunt. Next to him, Mother Wolf lay with her big grey nose on her four cubs. A bushy-tailed shadow fell across the cave.

It was the jackal Tabaqui. The wolves did not like Tabaqui. He was a mischief-maker and a gossip, and he stole scraps from the village trash. Still, Father Wolf let Tabaqui enter to look for food.

Tabaqui hurried in and began crunching on a bone. "Shere Khan is hunting nearby," the jackal told the wolf family.

Shere Khan was a tiger. He was born lame, but he was still powerful.

"He has no right," Father Wolf said. The wolves followed the Law of the Jungle. By that law, Shere Khan should have warned the other animals before changing his hunting grounds.

Tabaqui saw he was not welcome with the wolves. He slunk out of the cave.

The jungle echoed with the sound of a terrible snarl. It was Shere Khan, and he was hungry. "He will scare away all the deer with that noise!" said Father Wolf.

"He is not hunting deer," Mother Wolf said. "Tonight, Shere Khan is hunting man."

"Man!" cried Father Wolf with disgust.

Hunting man was off-limits. Men were weak, and it wasn't fair to kill them. Besides, whenever an animal killed a man, hundreds of people came soon afterward with torches and guns. Then every creature in the jungle had to pay.

The wolf family listened to Shere Khan. They heard a howl of pain. Father Wolf peered out of the cave. Shere Khan had burned his paws on a woodcutter's fire.

"Something is coming up the hill," said Mother Wolf.

The bushes rustled. Father Wolf crouched down. He sprang forward, then stopped himself mid-leap.

Right in front of him toddled a little boy, a man's cub. The boy was just old enough to walk. He looked up at Father Wolf and laughed.

Mother Wolf had never seen a man's cub.

"Bring it here," she said. Father Wolf lifted the boy in his jaws and brought him closer. The baby pushed its way in among the cubs to get warm.

"How bold!" said Mother Wolf.

Shere Khan and Tabaqui came to the mouth of the cave. "A man's cub came this way," growled Shere Khan. "Give it to me." The white tiger could not fit into the cave to take the boy himself.

Father Wolf shook his head. The man's cub belonged to the wolves now. It was up to the pack to decide what happened to it.

Shere Khan could not believe the wolves would go against his demands. "It is I, Shere Khan, who speaks!" he said.

"And I answer!" said Mother Wolf. She had once been the fiercest wolf in the pack. Now she was her old self again, dangerous and ready to protect her family to the death. "The man's cub is mine. He will run with the pack and hunt with the pack. And someday, Shere Khan, he will hunt *you*!"

Shere Khan knew he could not win a fight against Mother Wolf. "Let's see what the pack has to say about this," he said as he left the cave.

"It's true, we will have to show the cub to

the pack," said Father Wolf when the tiger was gone. "Are you sure you want to keep him?"

"Of course I want to keep him," Mother Wolf said. Then she turned to the child and spoke soft, motherly words to him. "I will call you Mowgli, the Frog."

# Chapter 2

Mowgli spent the next several weeks with the wolf family. He ate and slept with the wolf cubs. When the other cubs were old enough to run, Father Wolf brought them all to the Pack Council. All wolf cubs had to go to the council and be accepted by the pack. It was the Law of the Jungle.

The council was held on a hill full of rocks and places for the wolves to hide. The leader, the big grey wolf Akela, lay stretched out on a rock. Below him were all the other wolves. The cubs of the pack were in the middle, tumbling and playing where the wolves could see them.

Once in a while, an older wolf came closer to sniff the cubs. Parents nudged the shyer cubs forward so that they, too, would be noticed. "Look well, wolves!" said Akela.

Father Wolf pushed Mowgli forward with the other cubs. Mowgli was laughing and playing, right at home. None of the wolves made any comment.

Then a great roar boomed from behind the rocks. "The cub is mine!" Shere Khan called out. "Give him to me! What do the wolves have to do with a man's cub?"

Akela ignored Shere Khan. "Look well," he said again. "It is for us to decide what is a wolf's business."

But some of the wolves thought Shere Khan

had a good point. "What *do* we have to do with a man's cub?" one of them asked.

When the wolves disagreed about whether a cub should be accepted into the pack, the Law was clear. Two members of the council besides the cub's parents had to speak for it.

"Who will speak for this cub?" asked Akela.

For several moments there was no answer. Then Baloo the bear spoke up.

Baloo was an old brown bear who taught all the wolf cubs the Law of the Jungle. He was allowed at the council because he was wise and because he did not compete with the wolves for food. He ate nuts, berries, and honey, and he did not hunt.

"There is no harm in a man's cub," said Baloo. "Let him run with the pack, and I will teach him."

"Who else will speak for him?" asked Akela.

Out of the shadows slid a black shape. It was the panther Bagheera. He was brave and crafty, and the wolves were wary of him. Yet when he spoke, his voice was soft and sweet.

"I have no right to speak at your council,"

Bagheera purred. "But I do know the Law of the Jungle. I know that if there is a disagreement over a cub, the cub can be bought." Bagheera offered the wolves a fat bull that he had just killed. They were welcome to eat the bull if they would take Mowgli into the pack.

Most of the wolves thought Mowgli could not survive life as a wolf. They thought he would burn in the sun or freeze in the cold winter rains. What harm would it be to let him into the pack?

When he heard the way the council was leaning, Shere Khan roared with anger.

Akela was glad. "Men are wise," he said. "Mowgli may be a help to us someday."

So, for the price of a bull, Father and Mother Wolf were allowed to raise Mowgli as their own.

# Chapter 3

As time passed, Mowgli became more and more a part of life in the jungle. He could swim like a fish and run like a wolf. He plucked thorns out of the other wolves' feet. His brother and sister wolf cubs grew up and went out on their own. Then more brothers and sisters were born. Yet still Mowgli was a cub, with lots of growing up to do.

Besides Mother and Father Wolf, Mowgli spent the most time with Baloo the old brown bear and Bagheera, the panther who had bought his life at Council Rock. He liked to climb on Bagheera and watch him hunt. Bagheera loved Mowgli and called him Little Brother. He would have spoiled the boy if Baloo had let him.

Baloo kept his promise and taught Mowgli the Law of the Jungle. Because Mowgli was a man's cub and learned fast, Baloo did not stop with the lessons that he taught the other wolf cubs. He went on teaching. Soon Mowgli knew the languages of the birds and the snakes and many of the other creatures in the jungle.

Often Bagheera would come to lean against a tree and watch Mowgli's lessons.

"What is the Strangers' Hunting Call?" Baloo quizzed Mowgli one day.

"Please let me hunt here, because I am hungry," Mowgli recited.

"And what is the reply?" Baloo asked.

"Hunt, then, for food, but not for pleasure," said Mowgli.

"Now tell Bagheera the jungle greeting I taught you," Baloo said.

"The greeting for which creatures? I know *all* the languages," Mowgli said with a toss of his head.

"You know a little, but not much," said Baloo. He rolled his eyes. "See, Bagheera? They never thank their teacher." Baloo looked back at Mowgli. "Say the greeting for the bears, then, great scholar," he teased.

"We are one people, you and I," Mowgli growled like a bear.

"And the birds?" said Baloo.

"We are one people, you and I," Mowgli trilled.

"And the snakes?" Baloo asked.

"We are one people, you and I," Mowgli hissed. He kicked up his heels and clapped for himself. Then he jumped on Bagheera's back and made faces at Baloo.

"We're not finished," Baloo said.

Mowgli sighed loudly. "I'm tired of all this reciting," he said.

"The way to learn is to repeat the words over and over," said Baloo. "Now give me the Strangers' Hunting Call again."

"I just did that," Mowgli complained.

"Do it again," said Baloo.

Mowgli scowled. "Why should I listen to you, silly old bear?" he asked.

Baloo swatted Mowgli with his big paw. For a second, Mowgli froze. Then he turned and stormed off into the jungle.

"Baloo!" Bagheera protested. "Mowgli is so small."

"Is anything in the jungle too small to be hurt?" Baloo asked. "It is because he is little that he must learn so much. It will protect him."

Mowgli had gone to sit by himself against a tree. His head was bent, and he pounded his fist in the dirt. Now and then, he paused to feel the bruised spot where Baloo had hit him.

A furry grey head appeared in front of him, hanging upside down from the tree. Then another and another. Mowgli stared. He had never seen anything like these creatures before.

The three strangers dropped down and surrounded Mowgli. They walked upright like

Mowgli did, but they had long tails that they used almost like extra arms.

"Who are you?" Mowgli asked.

"We are the Bandar-log, the Monkey People," one of them said. "Hasn't Baloo told you about us?"

Mowgli shook his head.

"Well, we know about you," one of the other monkeys said.

The third monkey nodded. "We've seen the way Baloo works you all day long. We don't think it's fair," he said.

"We think you deserve better," said the first monkey.

"Come play with us!" more monkeys called from the trees.

"All right," said Mowgli.

The three monkeys picked Mowgli up and

carried him to the tops of the trees. "Come meet our new friend!" they cried to the rest of the Bandar-log.

More Monkey People came. They brought Mowgli nuts and other good things to eat. They giggled and chattered and played.

"Do you have lessons?" asked Mowgli.

"No!" the monkeys answered.

"Do you have lots of rules?" Mowgli asked.

"No!" cried the Bandar-log.

Mowgli smiled. "You're fun!" he said.

Soon Mowgli heard Baloo and Bagheera calling, "Mowgli! Little Brother!" Mowgli knew he had to go.

"Please take me back," he said.

The Bandar-log picked Mowgli up and brought him down through the trees and almost to the ground.

"Goodbye, friend! Come back and play with us again!" they cried.

Mowgli slid down a tree trunk and landed next to Baloo and Bagheera. "I came for Bagheera and not for you, fat old Baloo," he said.

"Fine with me," Baloo said, pretending as well as he could that he wasn't hurt.

Mowgli jumped up onto Bagheera's back. He tugged on the panther's fur and kicked at his shoulders excitedly.

"Watch my ribs, Little Brother," Bagheera said. "Why all this dancing up and down?"

"I am going to have a tribe of my own and lead them through the branches all day long," Mowgli bragged.

"What are you talking about, little dreamer of dreams?" Bagheera asked.

"*And* I'm going to throw branches and dirt at Baloo," Mowgli went on. "My new friends promised."

"Mowgli," Baloo growled. "Have you been talking to the Bandar-log?"

Mowgli looked at Bagheera for support, but the panther's eyes were as hard as jade stones. "Yes," Mowgli said to Baloo, a little less boldly. "Why haven't you ever told me about them?"

"The Bandar-log?" said Baloo with disgust. "There is a good reason why I have never spoken to you about the Bandar-log. They do not follow the Law of the Jungle. They have no laws!"

"They wanted to make me their leader," Mowgli said.

"They have no leader," said Bagheera. "They lie. They have always lied."

"It is shameful to speak with them," Baloo said sternly.

Mowgli hung his head. The Bandar-log were fun, but he knew that Baloo and Bagheera were his true friends. Together, the bear, the boy, and the panther settled down for a rest in the sun.

High above them up in the treetops, the Bandar-log watched them. The Monkey People liked Mowgli. So when he and his friends were fast asleep, the Bandar-log swung down from the trees.

Mowgli awoke to the feeling of being grabbed by the arms and legs. Quickly the monkeys swung him up high into the trees. The Monkey People screeched and howled with victory.

As they carried Mowgli away, Baloo woke

and realized what had happened. The great bear's roar shook the jungle. Bagheera dashed up the tree, snarling and showing his teeth. But the Bandar-log swept Mowgli higher and higher. They swung through the trees as easily as Mowgli could run through the jungle.

At first, Mowgli liked the wild ride. Soon, though, he began to feel sick. Through the branches, he glimpsed the ground far below

him. And all the while, over the miles of trees they swung through, the monkeys hooted and hollered.

He knew he was traveling much faster than Baloo and Bagheera could possibly follow. They would soon lose his trail. Mowgli had to get word to them. He looked up and saw Rann the kite flying high above the trees. He greeted the great bird in his own language.

"We are one people, you and I," Mowgli called. He was glad Baloo had taught him all the languages of the jungle. "Please help me. Watch where they take me! Then get word to Baloo and Bagheera."

Before Rann could answer, the monkeys leapt away, and Mowgli was gone.

Finally the monkeys stopped in a strange place. Mowgli had never seen anything like it. It was an abandoned city, ruined and over-grown. Trees and vines grew in and out of the walls. Up on a hill were the remains of a palace. Mowgli looked around with wide eyes.

The Bandar-log called the place their city. They ran freely about it, but they had no idea what all the buildings were for. They just climbed and played and shook the orange trees for the fun of watching the oranges fall.

The monkeys never seemed to rest. They joined hands and danced around, singing silly songs.

By now Mowgli was very hungry. "I am a stranger in this part of the jungle. Please bring me food or let me hunt here," he said.

"Yes, yes," the monkeys chattered. Twenty or thirty of them rushed off to find nuts and fruit for him, but then they squabbled over the food. In the end, none of it ever made it back to Mowgli.

"All Baloo said about the Bandar-log is true," Mowgli said to himself. He felt he had reached a very bad place indeed.

# Chapter 4

**B**aloo and Bagheera ran through the jungle. They had not stopped since the Bandar-log took Mowgli. Baloo remembered that sometimes Kaa the rock python fed on monkeys. He might know where to find them.

"What makes you think Kaa will help us?" Bagheera asked the bear.

"If he is hungry, we can promise him food," Baloo said.

"If he just ate, he will sleep for a month," said Bagheera. "He may be asleep now."

"We have to try," said Baloo.

They found Kaa stretched out in the sun. He was huge—thirty feet long at least—with mottled brown and yellow skin and a blunt nose. He had just shed his old skin, and the new one shone in the afternoon light. Bagheera and Baloo could tell the snake was hungry.

They came up to him carefully. "Good hunting," Baloo greeted him.

"Good hunting for us all," Kaa replied politely. "I am hungry. Have you seen any animals to hunt?"

"Not yet, but we are looking," said Baloo.

"Let me come with you," Kaa urged. "Hunting is easy for the two of you, but I have to climb through the trees and wait for days to catch a good meal. And the branches aren't as strong as they used to be. On my last hunt, I almost fell. As I slipped through the branches, the sound woke the Bandar-log. They laughed and called me evil names."

"Like footless yellow earthworm," Bagheera murmured.

"They called me *that*?" Kaa hissed.

"I heard them say something like it once," Bagheera said, "but I never listen to them."

Baloo hesitated. He didn't like having anything to do with the Monkey People, but he knew they had to rescue Mowgli.

"It is the Bandar-log we're after now," he finally admitted.

"Really? They must have done something terrible to put you on their trail," Kaa hissed.

Bagheera and Baloo told Kaa about Mowgli. They told how they had spoken for the boy at Council Rock and how much they cared for him. They told him that the Bandar-log had snatched Mowgli up and away into the treetops.

"This is not good," Kaa said. "Mowgli may be their pet now, but they will turn on him. Your man cub is not safe. The Bandar-log fear me more than anyone else. I will help you get Mowgli back. Where did they take him?"

Baloo frowned. "We don't know. We hoped you might have an idea, Kaa."

"Me?" Kaa said. "I do not hunt the Bandar-log. I will eat them if they cross my path, but I don't go looking for them."

Just then a voice called out, "Hello! Baloo, look up here!" It was Rann the kite.

"I spoke to Mowgli," Rann went on. "The Bandar-log have taken him to the Lost City. He asked me to find you and let you know."

Baloo chuckled with pride. Mowgli had remembered his lessons!

"Thank you," Bagheera said to Rann. "Next time I hunt, I will save some for you."

Bagheera, Baloo, and Kaa set off for the Lost City. Bagheera and Kaa traveled quickly. Baloo went at his own pace.

Meanwhile, Mowgli had made his own plans. He paced back and forth through the city, shouting out the Hunting Call, but he got no answer. He began to pace closer and closer to the city wall. When he thought he was close enough, he made a quick dash to the wall.

The monkeys pulled him back. "You don't know how lucky you are to be with us," they told him. They pinched him. Then they brought him to a decaying marble terrace.

"We are wonderful!" the Bandar-log said. "We are the most wonderful people in the jungle!" By the hundreds, the monkeys sang their own praises to Mowgli.

Overhead, a cloud was moving toward the moon. In the minute of deeper darkness, Mowgli might have a chance to escape.

At last the cloud blocked out the moon's

light. Mowgli was about to make a move when he heard a familiar light step on the terrace. It was Bagheera!

Swiftly and quietly, the panther struck at the crowd of monkeys around Mowgli. When they saw what was happening, the monkeys swarmed all over Bagheera. They bit him, scratched him, and pulled his hair.

As Bagheera struggled, five or six of the monkeys grabbed Mowgli. They dragged him to the top of a ruined summerhouse. They pushed him through a hole in the dome.

It was fifteen feet down. For most boys, it would have been a very bad fall. But Baloo had trained Mowgli well. He landed light on his feet.

"Stay there until we've killed your friend," the monkeys shouted down to him. "We'll play

again later . . . if the poisonous snakes don't get you."

Poisonous snakes? The summerhouse must be full of cobras! Mowgli heard rustling and hissing all around him. Quickly, he greeted them in their own language. "We are one people, you and I," he hissed.

The cobras relaxed. "Stand still so you don't step on us," they said.

Mowgli stood as still as he could. He strained his ears to listen to how the fight was going. There was chattering and scuffling, and he could hear Bagheera cough as he bucked and twisted under the attack of the monkeys.

Mowgli shouted to him, "Roll to the water tanks, Bagheera! Jump in the water!"

Bagheera heard Mowgli's shout. He slowly fought his way to the water.

Suddenly the Lost City echoed with a great, furious cry. Baloo had arrived! "Bagheera, I am here!" he bellowed. "Just wait till I get ahold of you, Bandar-log!"

As he reached the terrace, a wave of monkeys covered Baloo. He squeezed some of them tightly to his body, then began batting the others in a steady rhythm.

Bagheera finally reached the water tank. He threw himself in with a splash. It was too deep for the monkeys. They crowded around the tank, dancing up and down with rage. The panther struggled to keep his head out of the water. He looked around for Kaa. He was afraid the python had changed his mind.

The confusion grew. Baloo went on fighting. Mang the bat flew back and forth and broadcast the news of the battle to the whole jungle. Hathi the elephant trumpeted. More monkeys rushed in to help the others.

Then, with a clatter of loose stones, Kaa snaked over the wall. He came on fast, striking out at monkeys as he went.

"It is Kaa! Run!" the monkeys screeched. What Kaa had told Baloo and Bagheera was true—the Bandar-log *did* fear Kaa more than any other creature. They scattered. They climbed higher up the walls and trees, shrieking, watching for what would happen next.

Bagheera was out of breath from his fight and his struggle in the water. "Get the man cub and go," he panted. "They may attack again."

"They will not move till I let them," hissed Kaa. "Where is the man cub?"

"Here!" cried Mowgli from the ruins. "I'm trapped! I can't climb out."

"Take him away," called the cobras from the hole. "He dances like Mao the peacock. He will crush our babies."

Kaa laughed. "He has friends everywhere, this Mowgli," he said. "Stand back! I am going to break down the wall." He smashed the wall of the summerhouse with his nose, putting all his long, powerful body behind it.

In a cloud of dust, the wall gave way. Mowgli burst out and flung himself at Baloo and Bagheera. He put one arm around each of them.

"Are you hurt?" Baloo asked.

"I am hungry, sore, and bruised," Mowgli said. "But look at the two of you! They hurt you much more. You're bleeding."

"There is someone else who fought for you, Little Brother," said Bagheera. He pointed to the great python. "Here is Kaa. You owe your life to him."

Mowgli thanked Kaa. He promised that someday he would help the python in any way he could. "Good hunting," he said.

"You have a brave heart," Kaa said. "But go away with your friends now. You don't need to see what will happen next."

His friends should have listened to Kaa. Instead, Baloo went down to the water tank to get a drink. Bagheera smoothed his fur.

Kaa glided into the center of the terrace. He shut his jaws with a snap, and all the monkeys looked at him. "Do you see me?" Kaa asked.

"We see!" cried the monkeys.

"Now watch the Dance of the Hunger of Kaa!" the python hissed.

He began slithering in slow circles. He

looped and coiled in figure eights. The monkeys were entranced. Even Bagheera and Baloo froze.

"Come closer," Kaa hummed.

The monkeys moved closer. Baloo and Bagheera, too, drew nearer to Kaa.

Only Mowgli did not fall under the spell. To him, Kaa was just making circles in the dust. He did not understand what was happening, but he could see his friends were caught in Kaa's trance.

Mowgli put one hand on Baloo and one on Bagheera. The panther and bear shook themselves as if they were waking from a dream.

"Come on. Let's go," Mowgli whispered.

So Mowgli, Baloo, and Bagheera slipped away into the jungle.

# Chapter 5

For almost all of Mowgli's childhood, life in the jungle was good. He helped drive game for the wolf pack and had plenty to eat. He had good friends to keep him company.

But one winter the rains did not come. Mowgli met Sahi the porcupine in a bamboo thicket. Sahi told him that the wild yams were drying up.

Everyone knew that Sahi was a picky eater, so Mowgli just laughed. "What difference does that make to me?" he said.

"Not much *now*," replied Sahi. "But we'll see what happens. Tell me, can you dive in the rock pool anymore?"

"No," said Mowgli. "The foolish water is all gone. I don't want to break my head."

"Your loss. A small crack might let in some wisdom," said the porcupine.

When Mowgli told Baloo what Sahi had said, the bear looked serious. "Hmm," he said, half to himself. "Let's just wait and see how the *mohwa* tree blossoms."

Spring came, but Baloo's favorite tree never bloomed. The heat crept into the jungle. Everything turned yellow, then brown, and finally black. The green weeds and mosses dried up. The hidden pools sank down and caked over.

Mowgli had never known what hunger meant until then. He scraped stale honey out of old, deserted beehives. He dug for grubs under the bark of the trees. Everyone in the jungle was starving.

But worse than the hunger was the thirst. The heat sucked up all the moisture. The only water left was the thin trickle that had been the Waingunga River.

One day Hathi the wild elephant saw a long, dry ridge of blue rock poke up from the center of the stream. Hathi was the oldest animal in the jungle, and he knew what he was looking at. It was the Peace Rock.

Hathi lifted up his trunk and trumpeted. He was calling the Water Truce. The deer, wild pig, and buffalo joined the call. Then Chil the kite flew far and wide, spreading the news.

The Water Truce meant that all animals, predators and prey, could go to the river safely

to drink. By the Law of the Jungle, nobody was allowed to hunt at the river during the Water Truce.

All that hot summer, the animals gathered at the river to drink and get as cool as they could. They were thin and starved. Mowgli, who had no fur to cover himself up, looked the worst. His hair was matted. His ribs stuck out.

One evening the animals came as usual to the river. Everyone talked about how bad things were. "Even men are dying," said a young sambar, a kind of Indian deer. "I have seen them lying still in their fields. We are all in this together. Soon, we will lie still, too."

"The river has dried up even more since yesterday," said Baloo.

"It will pass, it will pass," said Hathi, squirting water on his back and sides.

Baloo looked at Mowgli. "I'm afraid the man cub won't last much longer," he said.

"Man cub this and man cub that," rumbled a voice. Shere Khan, the lame tiger, had come down to drink and wash. As he dipped his face in the river, dark, oily streaks clouded the water. It was blood.

"Ugh! Shere Khan, what shame have you brought here?" said Bagheera.

"Man," bragged Shere Khan. "I killed one an hour ago."

All the animals trembled with disbelief. "Man!" they cried. "He has killed man!"

"Killing man at a time like this! Couldn't you find anything else to eat?" said Bagheera with disgust.

"I killed for choice, not for food," replied Shere Khan.

Hathi looked angrily at the tiger. "You *chose* to kill man?" he said.

"Yes. It was my night and my right," said Shere Khan. "You know what I mean, Hathi."

"Yes, I know," Hathi said. "But now that you've drunk your fill, go. The river is to drink, not to pollute. Only you would brag about your right at a time like this, when men and animals suffer together!"

Hathi's three sons stepped forward threateningly. Shere Khan did not dare question Hathi's order. He slunk back to his lair.

"What is this right Shere Khan was talking about?" Mowgli whispered to Bagheera. "I thought it was *always* shameful to kill a man."

"Ask Hathi. I do not know," said Bagheera.

Mowgli waited a minute. He was a little afraid to talk to the great elephant. But his curiosity was so strong that it gave him courage. "What is Shere Khan's right, Hathi?" Mowgli asked. The other animals echoed his question.

"It is an old tale," said Hathi, "a tale older than the jungle. Keep silence along the banks, and I will tell it.

"You know, children, that of all things, you most fear man," he began. There was a mutter of agreement. "And do you know why you fear man? This is why. In the beginning of the jungle, before anyone can remember, all the beasts walked together. No animal was afraid of another."

Hathi went on to tell the story of how the first tiger brought fear into the jungle. That fear was of man. The tiger was terrified of man, and it made him ashamed. He begged to have one night each year when he could walk among men unafraid.

"From then on, the tiger has had his one night," said Hathi. "He has always remembered the way man shamed the first of the tigers. So on his night, whenever the tiger sees man, he kills him."

Hathi looked around before finishing his story. "And only when there is a great fear over us all, as this drought has brought, can we of the jungle lay aside our little fears. Then we can meet together in one place, as we do now," he said.

"Man only fears the tiger for one night?" asked Mowgli.

"Yes," said Hathi.

"But Shere Khan kills men two or three times a month," Mowgli said.

"You're right," Hathi said. "But *those* times he springs from behind. He turns his face away, because he is afraid. Only on his one night does he go openly into the village and walk into the huts. And he never knows ahead of time what night will be his. He feels it come upon him when the moon rises. It could be any night of the year."

Mowgli knew then that Shere Khan was afraid of him. His fear made the white tiger ashamed. He would never let go of his feud with the man cub.

Finally the rains came again, just as Hathi had promised they would. The Water Truce was over. The leaves grew green and strong. The *mohwa* tree blossomed once more.

But Mowgli never forgot the lesson he learned that night at the dried-up river.

Shere Khan hated and feared men. No matter how often Mowgli called himself a wolf, Shere Khan could never think of him as anything but a man.

# Chapter 6

So the months and years passed, until Mowgli was about twelve years old. Akela, the leader of the wolf pack, was getting older, too. By the Law of the Jungle, a wolf could only lead the pack as long as he could lead the hunt.

Mowgli saw more and more of Shere Khan the tiger. Many of the young wolves in the pack were friends with Shere Khan. If Akela had been younger and stronger, he would never have allowed it.

The tiger was sly. He had gained the young

wolves' trust by giving them scraps of food. Then he flattered them. He said he was surprised that such fine hunters would let themselves be ruled by an old, dying wolf and a man's cub. The young wolves grew to hate Mowgli.

Bagheera warned Mowgli that Shere Khan was up to no good. He reminded him that Shere Khan had vowed to kill him someday.

Mowgli just laughed. "I have you and I have Baloo," he said carelessly. "Why should I be afraid?"

"This is no joke," said Bagheera. "Open your eyes! Shere Khan doesn't dare kill you here in the jungle, for fear of me and Baloo and your other friends. But Akela is getting old. Soon he will miss his target in the hunt, and he won't be the leader anymore. The young wolves listen to Shere Khan. He has taught them that a man's cub has no place in the pack. That is what they believe."

"But I was raised in the jungle!" Mowgli cried. "They are my brothers! I have pulled thorns from all their paws."

"You are still a man's cub," Bagheera said. "Someday you will have to go back to your own kind. I think Akela will soon fail at the hunt. Then the pack will turn against both of you."

Bagheera paused, then went on. "I have an idea. Go down to the valley where the men have their huts. Take some of the Red Flower they grow there. That will give you better protection than any of your friends can. Get the Red Flower."

Bagheera was talking about fire. The animals of the jungle were terrified of fire, and none of them dared to call it by its name.

"I will get some," Mowgli agreed, unafraid.

"Good," said Bagheera. "Keep some in a pot for whenever you have need of it."

Mowgli darted away through the jungle. Suddenly he heard a howl that made him stop in his tracks. It was the wolf pack's hunt. He listened to the voices of the young wolves.

"Spring, Akela!" they said.

Mowgli heard the snap of teeth and a yelp. Akela had missed! He had failed at the hunt, just as Bagheera had predicted!

Mowgli didn't wait to hear anything else. He dashed on as fast as he could.

Soon he reached the fields where men grew their crops. He crept up outside one of their huts. He looked through the window and watched the fire in the fireplace. Night fell, and still Mowgli watched. He saw that the people looked very much like him.

In the middle of the night, a woman got up and fed the fire with black lumps. In the morning, a child picked up a clay pot and filled it with red-hot charcoal. The child carried the

pot outside when he went to milk the cows.

"Is that all?" said Mowgli. "If a cub can do it, I can do it." He walked boldly around the hut. He came face to face with the child and quickly took the pot from the boy's hand.

Then Mowgli disappeared into the mist.

# Chapter 7

**W**hen he was hidden again in the jungle, Mowgli stopped and looked at the pot of fire. He blew on it like he had seen the woman in the hut do. "This thing will die if I do not give it things to eat," he said to himself. He fed it some twigs and dried bark.

Soon, Mowgli met Bagheera, who had come in search of him. The morning dew shone like moonstones on his black fur.

"Akela has missed," Bagheera said.

Mowgli, of course, had already guessed

this, but it was different to hear it was true.

"They would have killed Akela at Council Rock last night," Bagheera went on, "but they were looking for you."

"I was by the man huts. I am ready with the Red Flower. See?" Mowgli said. He held up the fire pot.

Bagheera backed up a step. "Good," he said. "Aren't you afraid?"

Mowgli shook his head and said, "Why should I be afraid? I think I even remember that before I was a wolf, I used to lie in front of the Red Flower. It was nice and warm."

"Well, I have seen men put a dry branch into a pot like that, and the Red Flower bloomed at the end of it," said Bagheera.

Mowgli went home to the cave. All day, he practiced putting branches into the coals. He tried many different kinds of wood until he found the one that worked best.

In the evening, Tabaqui came and told him that he was wanted at the council. Mowgli laughed in his face, to show he was not afraid. And when he came to Council Rock, he was still laughing.

Instead of sitting on top of the rock, Akela lay next to it. This was a sign that the leadership was open. Shere Khan walked among the wolves.

Mowgli sat down with the fire pot hidden snugly between his knees. Bagheera lay next to him.

When Akela was in his prime, Shere Khan would never have dared talk at the council. Now he spoke freely.

"He has no right to speak here," Bagheera

growled softly to Mowgli. "Say something."

Mowgli jumped up. "Does Shere Khan lead the pack?" he asked. "The leadership of the pack is up to the pack to decide."

All the wolves began talking and shouting at once. "Quiet, man's cub!" said many of the younger ones. But the older ones said Mowgli had kept their law and had the right to talk.

Finally the oldest of the wolves said, "Let Akela speak!"

Akela looked tired. He knew that he would most likely not live through the night. He raised up his head and said, "I have led you for twelve years. Not once in that time has any wolf been hurt or trapped. Now you have the right to kill me here on Council Rock. So who will do it? By the Law of the Jungle, it is my right to make you fight me one by one."

The wolves were quiet. Akela was old, but still strong. None of them wanted to face him alone.

Then Shere Khan broke the silence with a loud roar. "Who cares about this old fool? I want to talk about the man's cub. He has troubled us for far too long. He should have been mine ten years ago. Give him to me."

More than half the pack howled in agreement. "Yes! He's a man! What does he have to do with us? Let him go to the other men."

"No!" Shere Khan snarled. "He would turn all the people in the village against us. Give him to me!"

Akela looked up again. "He has eaten our food. He has helped us hunt. He has kept the Law of the Jungle," he said.

"And I paid for him with a bull when he was

accepted," said Bagheera. "That may not mean much now, but my honor means everything to me. That is something I would fight for."

The wolf pack was in an uproar. Bagheera turned to Mowgli. "All we can do now is fight. It's up to you," he said.

Mowgli stood up with the fire pot in his hands. He looked brave, but inside he was angry and hurt. He'd had no idea the wolves felt that way.

"Listen!" he said. "You've called me a man enough tonight, even though I would have been a wolf with you my whole life. So you don't get to decide what happens next. I decide. Just in case you have any doubts about that—here! I have brought some of the Red Flower to convince you."

Mowgli threw the fire pot down. He stuck

his branch into the fire and whirled it over his head. The wolves backed away in terror.

"You're in charge now," Bagheera muttered. "Save Akela. He has always stuck up for you."

"Good," Mowgli said when he saw how Shere Khan and the wolves feared him. "Now that I know how you really feel, I'll go to live with my own people."

Mowgli walked straight up to Shere Khan. His burning branch threw sparks up into the darkening sky. Shere Khan closed his eyes for fear of the fire. "If you move, I'll shove this Red Flower down your throat!" Mowgli said. "Now go! But know that if I ever come back to Council Rock, it will be with your hide!"

Mowgli turned to the wolves. "You will let Akela go," he said. "Get out of here! I don't want to see your faces anymore!" He struck out at them with the fire, and the wolves ran away, howling.

When there was only Bagheera, Akela, and a few of the older wolves left, Mowgli began to cry. He sobbed and sobbed. He had never cried before and didn't even know what was happening to him.

"Let them fall, Mowgli. They are only tears," said Bagheera.

At last Mowgli stopped crying. He knew it was time to leave the jungle. "Before I go, I have to say goodbye to my mother," he said. So he went to the cave and snuggled against Mother Wolf and cried some more. The little wolf cubs howled.

"You won't forget me?" Mowgli asked his little brothers.

"Never," said the cubs. "When you're a man,

come to the bottom of the hill, and we'll talk to you."

"Come back soon!" said Father Wolf. "Your mother and I are old."

"Come soon!" Mother Wolf repeated.

"I will come," Mowgli promised. "And I will defeat Shere Khan. Don't forget me! Don't let anyone in the jungle forget me!"

So just before dawn, Mowgli went down the hillside to meet those mysterious things called men.

# Chapter 8

Mowgli had stolen the fire from the nearest village. But Mowgli felt it was too close to home and all his enemies. So he jogged twenty miles down the valley, where it opened onto a plain. At one end of it was another village. Mowgli had never seen this place before. He decided he had gone far enough.

Cattle and buffaloes were grazing all over the plain. When the herder boys saw Mowgli, they shouted and ran away. The village dogs began barking.

Mowgli was not afraid. He walked calmly along. He was hungry, and he wanted to get to the village and find something to eat.

A huge thorny bush stood beside the gate at the edge of the village. At night the villagers rolled it in front of the gate to keep the jungle animals out.

Mowgli sat down next to the gate. Soon a man came by. Mowgli stood up and opened his mouth. He pointed at it to show that he wanted food. The man ran away, startled.

The man came back with a priest and a crowd of people. They all shouted and stared and pointed at Mowgli. *These people have no manners,* thought Mowgli. *Only the Bandar-log would act like this.* He tossed his long black hair and frowned.

"There is nothing to be afraid of," said the

priest. "See the marks on his arms and legs? They are wolf bites. He is just a wolf child who has run away from his jungle."

If Mowgli could have understood the priest's words, he would have laughed. The other wolf cubs had nipped a little too hard sometimes in play, but Mowgli would never call it *biting.* He knew what real biting was.

"Poor child," some of the women said. "He is a handsome boy, with eyes like fire."

One of the women turned to her friend. "Messua, he looks like your boy who was taken by the tiger."

A woman with copper bracelets and anklets stepped forward to see Mowgli more closely. "He does," she agreed. "He is thinner, but he looks a lot like my son, Nathoo."

The priest looked up at the sky as if he

were searching for an answer from the heavens. "The jungle took away your son," he said to Messua. "Now it has given you this boy. Take him in and care for him."

Mowgli felt like he was being examined by the wolves once again. Would this man pack accept him?

Messua beckoned him to follow her.

They went to her hut. It was full of things that were strange to Mowgli—a red bed, copper pots and pans, a little statue of a Hindu god, and a shiny mirror.

Mowgli had never been under a roof before. It made him uneasy. Still Mowgli knew he would have to get used to it.

Messua gave Mowgli a drink of milk and some bread. Mowgli decided that if he was going to be a man, he would have to learn to talk like one. He began to point to things in the hut, and Messua gave him the words for them. Since Baloo had taught him the languages of all the animals, Mowgli learned quickly.

Bedtime did not go as smoothly. The thatched roof reminded Mowgli of a panther trap, and he would not sleep under it. As soon as Messua and her husband closed the door, Mowgli climbed out the window.

"Let him go," said Messua's husband. "He is used to sleeping outside. If he is meant to replace our lost son, he won't run away."

Mowgli stretched out on some long grass at the edge of the field. He closed his eyes, but a moment later, he felt a soft nose poking him under the chin. It was Grey Brother, the oldest of Mother Wolf's cubs!

"Phew!" Grey Brother said. "You smell like

cattle and wood smoke. You smell like a man already!"

Mowgli sat up. "Is everyone all right in the jungle?" he asked.

"Everyone except the wolves who were burned," said Grey Brother. "But listen. Shere Khan is embarrassed. He has gone away to hunt somewhere else until his scorched fur grows back in. He swears that when he comes back, he'll throw your bones in the river."

Someday, Mowgli knew, he would have to defeat Shere Khan. But he was too tired to think about it now. He thanked Grey Brother for the news.

"You won't forget you are a wolf?" Grey Brother asked. "Men won't make you forget?"

"Never," said Mowgli. "I will always remember that I love you and everyone in our cave.

But I can't ever forget I've been cast out of the pack, either."

"Men may cast you out of their pack, too," Grey Brother warned. "Men are only men, Little Brother."

For the next three months, Mowgli hardly left the village. He was too busy learning how to be a man. First, they made him wear strange clothing. He didn't like it. Then they tried to teach him about money. He could not understand the use of it.

The little children laughed at him when he said words wrong and because he wasn't interested in toys or games. Luckily for the children, the Law of the Jungle had taught Mowgli that it was unfair to hurt little cubs. He kept his temper under control.

In fact, Mowgli did not know his own

strength. He was weak compared to his animal friends, but to the villagers, he was as strong as a bull. He was also fearless.

Every evening the village headman, the watchman, the barber, and Buldeo, the village hunter, gathered on a platform under the fig tree. They sat and smoked. Above them in the tree, monkeys chattered, and under them, below the platform, lived a cobra.

The men settled in and began talking. They told wonderful tales of gods and men and ghosts. Then Buldeo began to tell stories about the beasts of the jungle. Mowgli, who knew better than anyone what the jungle was really like, tried hard not to laugh. Buldeo's stories were ridiculous!

Buldeo began talking about the tiger that had carried away Messua's son. He said it was a ghost tiger. He said that the spirit of a wicked old man named Purun Dass had taken over the tiger's body.

"I know this is true because Purun Dass walked with a limp. And this tiger has a limp, too," said Buldeo.

Buldeo was talking about Shere Khan! Mowgli had to say something. "Everyone knows that tiger limps because he was born lame. This is child's talk! Are all your stories such nonsense, such cobwebs and moon talk?"

Buldeo and the other elders of the village were shocked. "Oh, it's the jungle brat," Buldeo said. "Well, if you know so much about that tiger, get his hide! There's a reward of a hundred rupees to the one who kills that tiger. Now, settle down and don't talk when your elders are speaking."

Mowgli stood up to go. "I've been listening all night!" he shouted over his shoulder as he walked away. "Almost nothing Buldeo has said about the jungle is true—and the jungle is all around us! If I can't believe his stories, then why should I believe all the tales of ghosts and gods and goblins?"

Buldeo puffed and snorted.

"It is high time that boy was put to work," the headman said.

The people of the village decided Mowgli would go out the next day to herd the buffaloes. It was a good job for Mowgli. He wanted to be outside, away from this strange life among the men.

# Chapter 9

At dawn the next day, Mowgli rode through the village street on Rama, the great herd bull. The buffaloes woke up and followed him. He told the other herder children to take the cattle to graze on their own. Mowgli himself took charge of the buffaloes.

Buffaloes in India like to wallow in muddy places. Mowgli led them to the edge of the plain, where the Waingunga River left the jungle. Then he climbed down from Rama's back and went to a clump of bamboo. Grey Brother had promised to wait for him at this spot.

There he was! Mowgli and his brother greeted each other happily. It had been months since Mowgli had had any news from the jungle. "What is Shere Khan doing?" he asked.

"He came back looking for you," Grey Brother said. "He went away again because the hunting isn't good here right now. But he still says he will kill you."

Mowgli thought for a minute. "Okay," he said. He pointed to a large rock in the distance. "As long as he is away, you or one of the brothers sit on that rock every morning as I leave the village with the herd. When he comes back, wait for me in the ravine by the *dhâk* tree. Then we can make a plan."

After Grey Brother left, Mowgli settled down for a nap. Herding in India is very lazy work. The herdsboys doze or catch grass-hoppers or make mud castles. An afternoon seems as long as a whole lifetime.

Day after day, Mowgli led the herd out. Each morning, he saw Grey Brother far away on the rock, and he knew he was still safe from Shere Khan.

Then one day, Grey Brother wasn't there. Mowgli headed for the meeting place under the *dhâk* tree to find him.

"Shere Khan has been hiding for a month to throw you off track," Grey Brother said. "He crossed the ranges with Tabaqui last night, hot on your trail."

"I am not afraid of Shere Khan," Mowgli said, "but Tabaqui is very cunning."

"Don't worry about Tabaqui," said Grey Brother. "I attacked him last night. I found out all their plans. Shere Khan will be hiding at the village gate tonight. He is waiting now, in a big, dry ravine."

"Has he eaten?" Mowgli asked. He knew that if Shere Khan was hungry, he would be light and fast and very dangerous.

"He ate a pig at dawn, and he drank, too," Grey Brother said.

"What a fool!" Mowgli gloated. Shere Khan would be heavy and sluggish with a stomach full of food and water.

Mowgli tried to think of a plan. "The buffaloes would charge only if they caught his scent. I can't speak their language. Is there any way we could get the herd behind him so they can smell him?" he asked.

"He swam far down the river to hide his scent," said Grey Brother.

Mowgli considered this. If he got the buf-
faloes to charge down one end of the ravine,
Shere Khan could just sneak out the other end.
He would escape.

"Do you think you could divide the herd?"
Mowgli asked Grey Brother.

"Not by myself," he answered, "but I
brought help." Grey Brother walked away and
dropped down into a hole. A few seconds later,
a great grey head rose out of the hole with a
loud hunting howl.

"Akela! Akela!" Mowgli shouted, clapping
his hands. Now he knew they would get the job
done. "Akela, help me divide the herd. Put the
females and young calves in one group and the
bulls in another."

Akela and Grey Brother dashed into the
herd. They weaved in and out, driving the

females and calves to one side and the bulls to the other. The mother buffaloes were red-eyed and angry. The bulls were bigger, but Mowgli knew the protective mothers were more dangerous.

Mowgli told Akela to drive the bulls away to the left. "When we are gone," he said to Grey Brother, "drive the mothers and calves down to the foot of the ravine, until the sides of the ravine are higher than Shere Khan can jump. Keep them there till we come down."

Then Mowgli leapt onto Rama's back and followed as Akela led the bulls away. The wolf turned them toward the jungle.

Rama snorted and shook with anger.

"Oh! If I could only talk to Rama and tell him what I need him to do!" Mowgli said.

They led the bulls in a long, wide circle.

That way, Shere Khan could not smell the herd and figure out Mowgli's plan too soon. Finally Akela and Mowgli brought the bulls to the top of the ravine where the tiger rested. Grey Brother had led the mothers and calves to the other end of the ravine. If the plan worked, Shere Khan would be sandwiched in between.

Mowgli gave the bulls a minute to catch their breath. Then he put his hands up and called down the ravine. His voice echoed from rock to rock.

Shere Khan woke up with an angry snarl. "Who calls?" he asked.

"I, Mowgli! Shere Khan, it is time to come to Council Rock!" Mowgli shouted. "Go, Akela! Go, Rama! Bring them down!"

The bulls paused. Akela gave a great howl, and they began charging down the ravine.

In a few seconds, Rama caught Shere Khan's scent. He bellowed.

"Ha!" Mowgli yelled to the bull. "Now you understand!"

By now it was a full stampede. Foaming at

the mouth, the bulls crashed down the ravine. Weaker bulls were shouldered to the side as the strongest ones charged on.

Shere Khan heard the thunder of their hooves. He got up and lumbered in the other

direction. He looked at the sides of the ravine, but he could not find a way out. He moved as quickly as a tiger on a full stomach can.

The bulls bellowed when they reached the pool where Shere Khan had just been. The cows at the other end of the ravine gave an answering bellow. The tiger halted and turned. He was trapped!

Rama and the bulls came on like thunder. They trampled Shere Khan and kept running. The two parts of the herd met in a loud and furious mass.

"Break them up, Akela," Mowgli said. He jumped down from Rama's back. "Softly. Softly, my children," he said soothingly to the herd.

Between the three of them, Mowgli, Grey Brother, and Akela managed to calm the buffaloes. Mowgli gathered the herd together, then went to check on Shere Khan.

He was dead. "His hide will look good on Council Rock," said Mowgli. He quickly set to work skinning the tiger, a task no village man would think of doing alone.

After an hour or so, Mowgli felt a hand on his shoulder. It was Buldeo, the village hunter. The other herder boys had run back to the village and told everyone about the buffalo stampede. Buldeo had come out to scold Mowgli for not taking better care of the herd.

As soon as they saw the man, the two wolves ducked out of sight.

Buldeo had noticed what Mowgli was doing. "So the buffaloes killed a tiger?" he said. "What is this foolishness? You think you can skin it yourself? Look, it is the lame tiger! The one worth a hundred rupees." Buldeo paused. "Well, maybe I will overlook you letting the herd get away, since this happened. Maybe I will even give you one rupee from the reward."

Mowgli kept on skinning. "Hmm," he said, half to himself. "So you're going to take the hide from me, turn it in for the reward, and *maybe* give me one rupee? I think I'll keep the hide for myself, old man!"

Buldeo opened his mouth in shock. "How dare you speak like that to the chief hunter of the village?" he demanded. "You're not getting a bit of the reward. The only thing I'm giving you is a beating!"

Mowgli was still not impressed. He sighed. "Must I listen to you all day?" he asked. Then, in wolf talk, he said, "Akela, this man is getting on my nerves."

It seemed to Buldeo that the grey wolf rose up out of nowhere. Quickly, Akela knocked the hunter down and stood over him. Buldeo was terrified. A boy who commanded wolves must be a powerful sorcerer, he thought.

"Great king," Buldeo said to Mowgli, "I did not know that you were anything more than a herdsboy. May I get up and go now, or will this wolf tear me to pieces?"

"Go, then," said Mowgli. "But next time, don't interfere with me. Akela, let him go."

Buldeo hobbled back to the village as fast as he could.

Mowgli calmly went on with his work. It was almost dark before he finished. He picked up the tiger hide and called to Akela. "Help me herd them again, Akela," he said.

When Mowgli and Akela returned to the

village with the buffaloes, they saw lights. They heard a great racket of bells ringing and conches blowing. Mowgli was sure it was a celebration because he had killed Shere Khan. He went on proudly.

But then a stone whizzed by close to his face. And another. The villagers began shouting, "Sorcerer! Jungle demon! Go away!"

"They are like the pack, these brothers of yours," said Akela. "I think they are throwing you out."

"Wolf! Wolf's cub! Go away!" shouted the priest.

"Again?" said Mowgli. "Last time it was because I was a man. This time it's because I'm a wolf. Let's go, Akela."

Suddenly Messua broke out of the crowd and ran toward Mowgli. "Oh, my son!" she cried. "They say you are a sorcerer who can turn into a beast at will. I don't believe them. I know you killed the tiger that caused Nathoo's death. But go away, or they will kill you."

A stone hit Mowgli on the mouth. "Go back, Messua," he said. "This is just one of the silly tales they tell under the big tree at dusk. At least I have paid for your son's life. Goodbye!"

Messua hurried back to the village.

"Now, once more, Akela," Mowgli cried. "Bring the herd in."

Akela yelled, and the buffaloes charged through the gate like a whirlwind. The crowd scattered.

"Goodbye, children of men!" Mowgli cried.

He turned and walked away, with Grey Brother and Akela at his heels.

# Chapter 10

**D**awn was breaking when Mowgli and the two wolves made it home. They stopped at the cave first to see Mother Wolf.

"They have cast me out of the man pack, Mother," Mowgli called into the cave. "But I have brought Shere Khan's hide, just like I promised I would."

Mother Wolf came out of the cave with the cubs. She was getting old and walked stiffly, but her eyes lit up when she saw the skin. "I told him back then, when he crammed his head into this cave hunting you, that one day you would hunt him. Well done," she said.

"Well done, Little Brother," a deep voice said from the thicket. Bagheera came running toward Mowgli. "We were lonely without you."

They all climbed up to Council Rock together. Mowgli spread the tiger's skin out on the ground where Akela used to sit. Akela lay down on it and howled his old gathering call. "Look well, wolves!"

The pack had not had a leader since Akela, but they answered the call out of habit. One by one they came. Some were lame from falling into traps or being shot. Many were mangy. And there were fewer wolves than when Akela led the pack. But still they all came and saw Shere Khan's hide stretched out on Council Rock.

"Look well, wolves," Mowgli said. "Have I kept my word?"

"Yes," the wolves bayed.

"Lead us again, Akela. Lead us, man cub," one of the wolves begged. "We are sick of this lawlessness."

"No," Bagheera purred. "He can't trust you now. When you are fully fed and more comfortable, you could turn on him again. You fought for your freedom. Eat it, wolves."

"Man pack and wolf pack have cast me out," said Mowgli. "Now I will hunt alone in the jungle."

"We will go with you," said his four brother cubs.

So Mowgli and the four cubs went away to hunt on their own in the jungle.

As the years passed, Mowgli became a

great leader in the jungle. He had many adventures. He journeyed with Kaa to meet a white cobra who guarded treasure deep underground beneath the Lost City. He saved the jungle from the red hunting dog. And he never forgot the animals who had always loved him best—his wolf family, Akela, and most of all, the brown bear Baloo and Bagheera the panther, his bravest and truest friends.

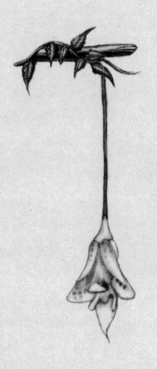

# About the Author

Rudyard Kipling was born in Bombay, India, in 1865, and when he was six years old, his parents took him to England. As an adult, he lived in India, England, South Africa, and even the United States. *The Jungle Book*, with its tales of Mowgli, Rikki-tikki-tavi, and the white seal, was first published in 1894. Kipling won the Nobel Prize in Literature in 1907. He died in 1936 and was buried in Poets' Corner in Westminster Abbey in London.

**If you liked this thrilling adventure,
you won't want to miss . . .**

# TREASURE ISLAND

### by **Robert Louis Stevenson**
### adapted by **Lisa Norby**

I scrambled onto the deck. Israel Hands lay nearby, alive but wounded.

"I am taking over the ship," I told him.

Mr. Hands looked up at me. "Very well, Captain Hawkins," he said. "I'll obey you. I have no choice."

For a few minutes I was so busy that I almost forgot that Mr. Hands was just pretending to be badly hurt. But all of a sudden something made me turn around. He had sneaked up behind me! He pulled out the knife. Then he charged.

# Swiss Family Robinson

### By Johann Wyss
### Adapted by Daisy Alberto

For many days our ship had been tossed at sea. The storm raged and raged. Above us, the seamen yelled frantically to each other.

My heart sank as I looked around the cabin at my family. My brave wife was trying to calm the children. Our four sons were filled with terror.

Suddenly I heard a cry. At the same time, the ship struck something! Water poured in on all sides.

"Lower the boats!" the captain shouted.

I rushed on deck. The last lifeboat was already pushing off!

# The Adventures of Tom Sawyer

### by Mark Twain
### adapted by Monica Kulling

The next day Tom and Huck walked back to the haunted house.

Inside was a dirt floor with weeds growing everywhere. The fireplace was crumbling. And cobwebs hung from the ceiling like curtains!

The boys climbed a rickety staircase to look upstairs. They peeked in a closet in the corner. But nothing was in it. As they turned to go back downstairs, Tom heard a noise.

The boys lay on the floor and peered through a knothole. Two men were entering the house!